W9-ACV-225

AUG 9 1
J

J
E
BAYLOR

Baylor, Byrd

Your own best se-
cret place

DUE DATE			
			(6-10)

YOUR OWN BEST
SECRET PLACE

BY BYRD BAYLOR AND PETER PARNALL

CHARLES SCRIBNER'S SONS · NEW YORK

1 3 5 7 9 11 13 15 17 19   RD/C   20 18 16 14 12 10 8 6 4 2
Library of Congress Cataloging in Publication Data
Baylor, Byrd.
Your own best secret place.
SUMMARY: Considers the pleasures to be found in one's very own private place, whether
it be a hollow in a tree, a sandy gully, or a secret sand dune.
I. Parnall, Peter.   II. Title.
PZ7.B3435Yo   [Fic]   78-21243
ISBN 0-684-16111-7

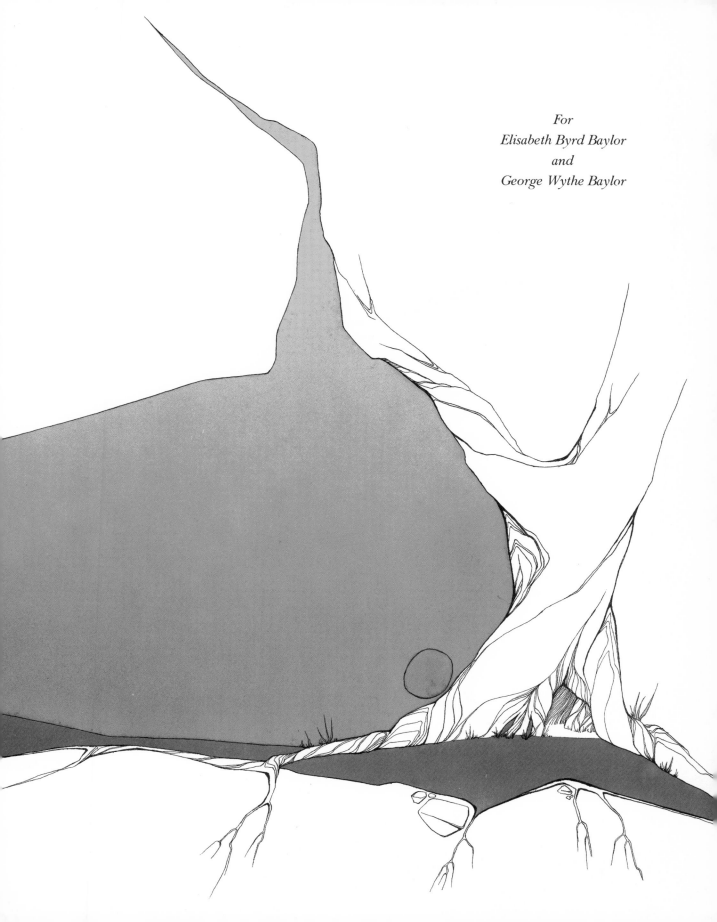

For
Elisabeth Byrd Baylor
and
George Wythe Baylor

His name is
William Cottonwood.

That's all
I know about him…
just that
and
the way
he loved
a secret place
he had to
leave.

I think of
William Cottonwood
a lot.

I wish I knew
where
he is
now.

I'd tell him
how
I found
his secret place

and how
I'm
taking care of it
and that
I hope
he doesn't mind
my being there.

Or
you
could tell him
for me.

If you ever meet
somebody
and his name is
William Cottonwood
and he used to live
by the Rio Grande River
in a valley
in New Mexico where
there are
chile farms
and cornfields…
then

ask him
if
he left
three messages
nailed up
on a hollow tree.

If he says
yes,
then he's
the William Cottonwood
I'm looking for.

Tell him
this
for me.

Just say
I found his place
by accident.

It was
early morning
on a rainy day.

I was on
the far side
of the river,
away
from the farms,
away
from the muddy
dirt road.

He must have walked there
too…
through
the same tangle of
shadowy thickets
and tall
river grass
and salt cedars
and willows
and cottonwood trees.

He must have liked
the damp
leaf smell
and the sudden
swoop of
piñon jays
and the long
straight
shafts of
sunlight
through the
treetops
there.

He must have heard
the same small owl
I always hear.

Maybe he
was like me,
sitting there
on a fallen white
tree trunk
wanting
beavers
or badgers
or a fox
to pass by.

He may have
found
his secret place
the same way
I did,

by climbing up on
that dead
fallen tree
and liking
the way
it makes a bridge

and balancing

and then
walking
the length
of its long
heavy trunk.

That's where I was
when
I noticed
a hollow
in the foot of
a cottonwood tree.

Then
I was down
on my hands and knees
looking in,
expecting to see—
maybe
fox tracks.

But what I saw was
a ragged
blue blanket
back there
in the hole
and
next to the blanket
a red coffee can.

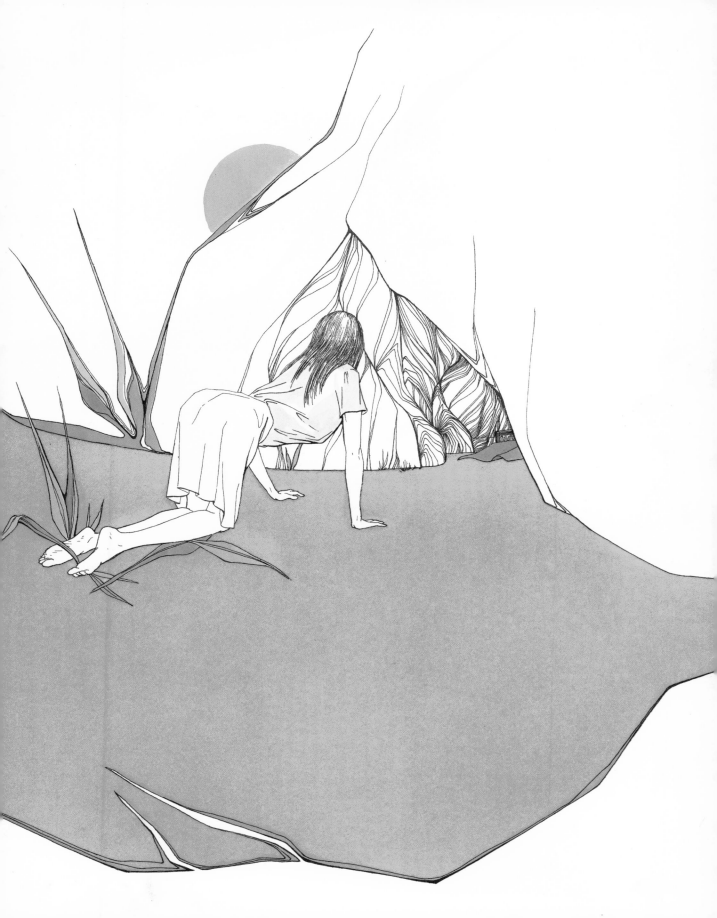

I thought I shouldn't
go inside
since
someone else's
things
were there.

I started to
leave.
That's when I saw
three notes
nailed up
on the tree.

You could tell
they were written
on brown paper sacks
he had cut
into squares.

IF ANYBODY FINDS MY PLACE READ THIS

I HAVE TO GO AWAY BUT I WILL BE BACK
NO MATTER WHAT

IF YOU ARE COLD YOU CAN USE THE BLANKET

BUT DO NOT USE MY OTHER STUFF

KEEP IT IN THE TREE
KEEP IT DRY
SIGNED WILLIAM CRUZ

NO MATTER HOW LONG I AM GONE
THIS IS STILL MY TREE

TO MAKE SURE I REMEMBER IT
I CHANGE MY NAME FROM WILLIAM CRUZ
TO WILLIAM COTTONWOOD

EVERYONE SHOULD CALL ME WILLIAM COTTONWOOD

BEGINNING NOW
SIGNED
WILLIAM COTTONWOOD

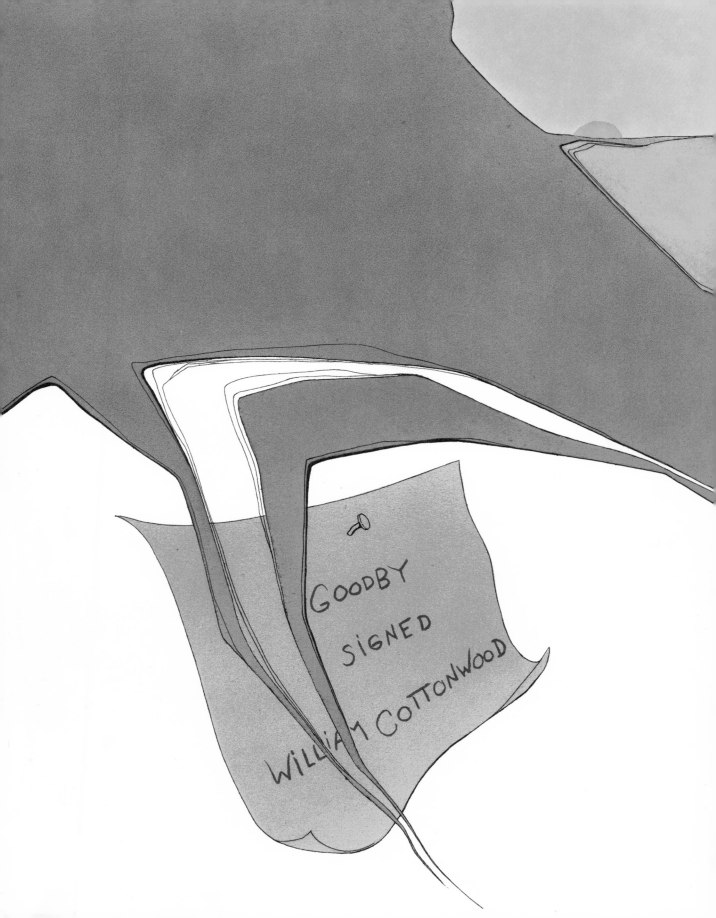

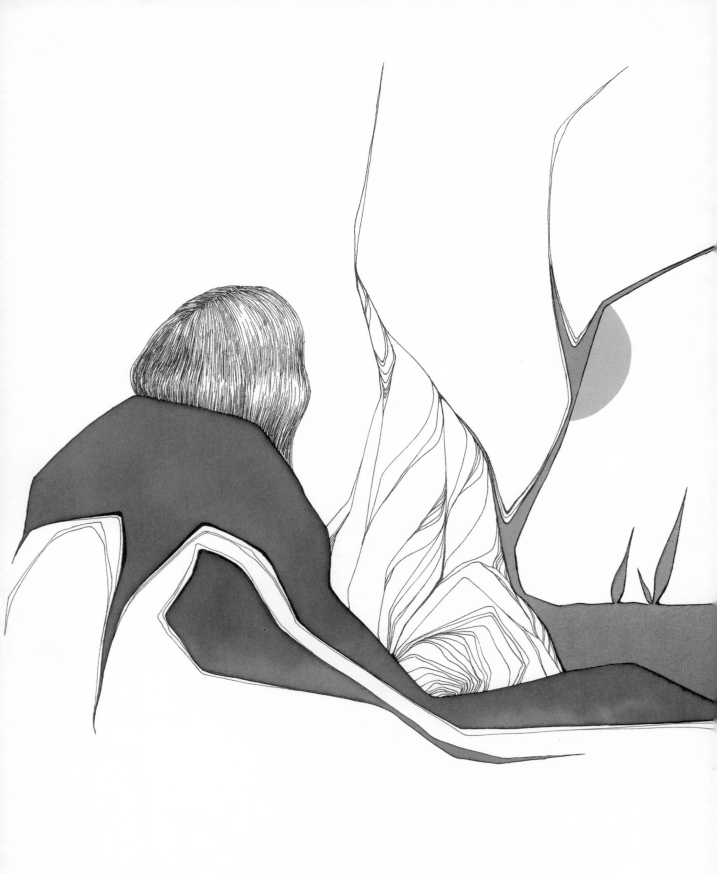

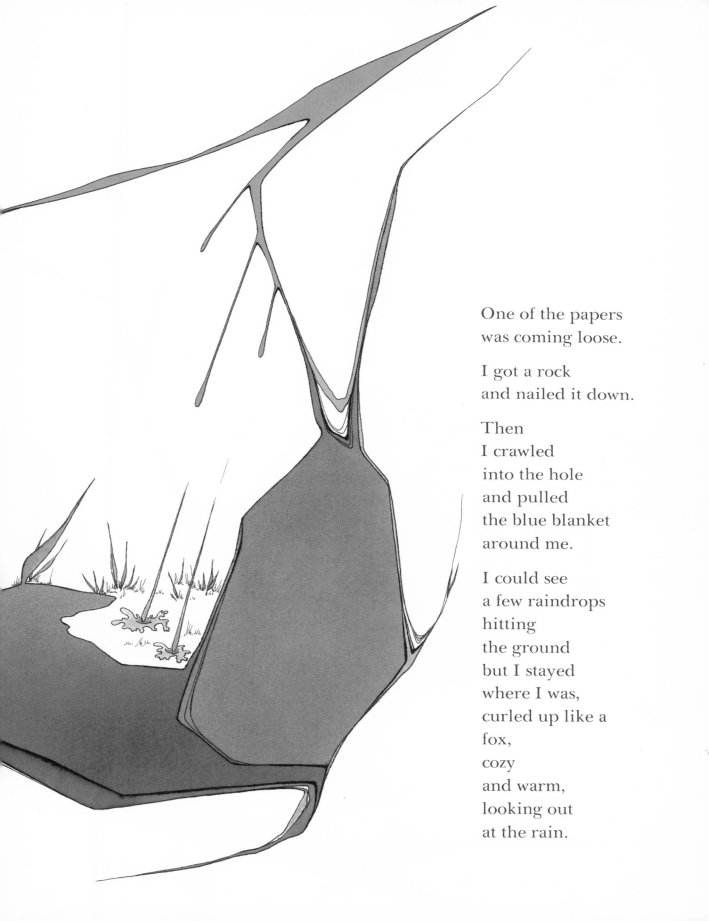

One of the papers
was coming loose.

I got a rock
and nailed it down.

Then
I crawled
into the hole
and pulled
the blue blanket
around me.

I could see
a few raindrops
hitting
the ground
but I stayed
where I was,
curled up like a
fox,
cozy
and warm,
looking out
at the rain.

I began
to understand
how
William Cottonwood
felt there.

Then
it seemed like we
were
friends
and maybe
he'd want me
to look
at the things
he had left
in that red
coffee can—

so I did.

They were all
good things:

the stub of a pencil,
a knife with two blades,
a candle burned down
almost to the end,
a feather I liked,
and a picture he'd drawn
on a sack.

It was a picture of
what
you see,
looking out.

I held it up
and it was
right.

He had put in
a rabbit too.
I knew how
quiet
that rabbit
must have sat
while
William Cottonwood
was drawing.

I never looked
in the can again.

At first
I used to wonder
why
he left
those things.

I knew he didn't
forget
them.

What I think is
that
leaving
things you like
means
you'll be back.

I think of
William Cottonwood
a lot.

And
sometimes,
sitting in his tree,
I think of
other
private
hidden
secret places
I have had.

The best one
was
a place
I used to go
when I was
little.

SOULE BRANCH LIBRARY

It was just
a sandy gully
cutting through
the hard
flat
Texas earth,
but that gully
was
a whole world
by itself
and I was
the only
person
there.

It was more like
a ditch
than a canyon
but
I'd never seen
a canyon
then
and it was
what
I thought
a canyon
ought
to be.

It was
deep
and wide
and the walls
were
taller
than I was,
and when
I looked up
I could only see
sky.

I always
had to
run
there.

I *had* to
lift
my arms up
high.

I *had* to be
barefoot
even if
sand
was burning
my feet.

Since then
I've seen
a hundred
deeper canyons
but
I still miss
that gully
that wasn't
even
a canyon
at all.

I know
William Cottonwood
would like it
there.
If I could,
I'd let him
borrow it
awhile
until
he goes home
to his tree.

But
nobody
knows
where he is.

I've told
a few people
about him.

One was a boy
who has a place
where
fifty bales of hay
are stacked up
in a barn.

He says those
fifty bales of hay
make
mountains
and tunnels
and craters
and caves.

He says
mice
play
all around him
and they aren't
afraid.

He says
hay
smells better than
flowers
and is the best thing
in the world
to sleep on.

And he says
he'll share
that place
with William Cottonwood
if William Cottonwood
is in
Montana.

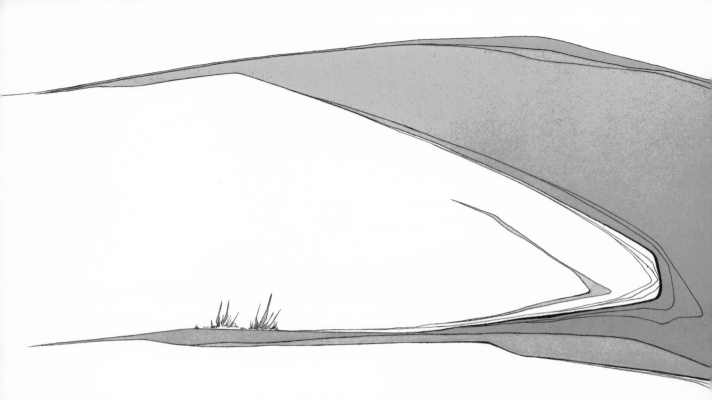

I told
two girls.

The place they like
is a white
sand dune.

It's out
in the open,
not hidden away
like
secret places
usually are,
but
nobody
goes there
but them.
It's
private
in a different way.

They say
any little wind
makes
ripples
there
and the sand
all looks like
waves
and
changes
every day
and always seems
magic.

They say
they'll share
with William Cottonwood.
Their sand dune
is five miles down the road
from Yuma, Arizona.

Somebody else I know
has a pear tree
in Virginia
that bends
down
to the ground.
He sleeps there
lots of times
on summer nights
and
eats
a pear
for breakfast.

He told me
he would
ask around
for
William Cottonwood.

You can too.

If you find him
and you take him
to your own
best
secret
place,
then
while you're
sitting there
together

just tell him this
for me.

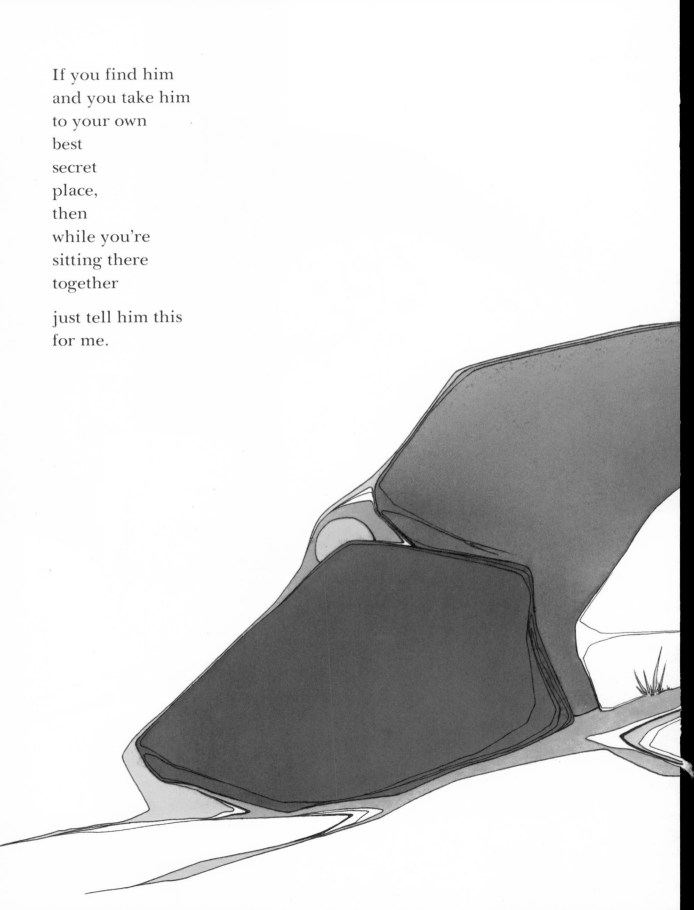

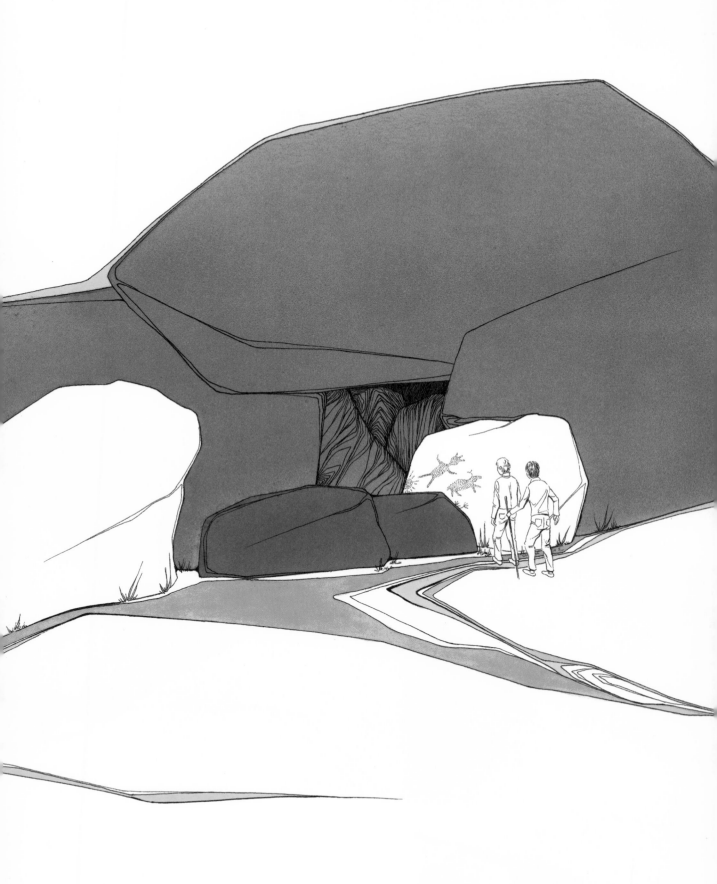

Say
I keep a list
of all the
birds
and animals
I see
from where I sit
inside his tree,
looking out.

Say I've brought
another
coffee can.
I keep the list
in it.
It's there
for him to read
when he
comes home.

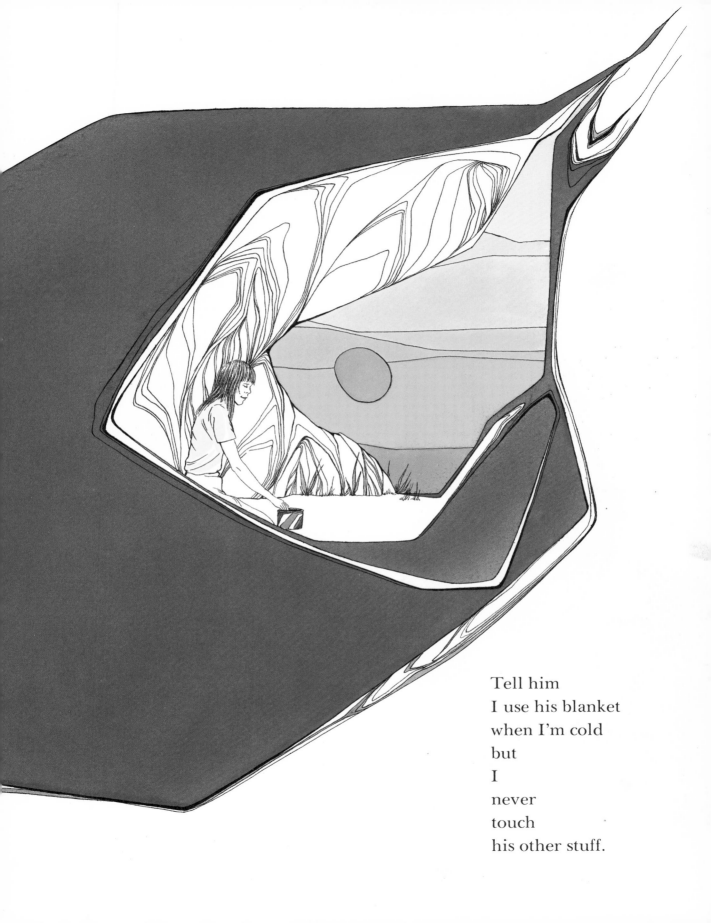

Tell him
I use his blanket
when I'm cold
but
I
never
touch
his other stuff.

Tell him
I think of him
a lot.

Tell William Cottonwood
I'm
here.

Byrd Baylor and Peter Parnall have
collaborated on three Caldecott
Honor books: *The Desert Is Theirs;*
Hawk, I'm Your Brother; and
The Way To Start a Day.

Byrd Baylor lives in the Southwest.
Her eloquent lyric prose reflects a
philosophy as special and lovely as
the lands she writes about. For her it
is the spirit—not material things—
that is necessary for personal
development. "Once you make that
decision, your whole life opens up
and you begin to know what matters
and what doesn't."

Peter Parnall lives on a farm in
Maine with his wife and two
children. His drawings have been
described as stunning, glittering, and
breathtaking. When he draws the
animal world, he has an uncanny
ability to portray that world as the
animals themselves might
experience it.